Giada De Laurentiis's
Recipe for Adventure
Philadelphia!

written with Brandi Dougherty
illustrated by Francesca Gambatesa

Grosset & Dunlap
An Imprint of Penguin Random House

Dedicated to mom and daughter adventures.

GROSSET & DUNLAP

Penguin Young Readers Group

An Imprint of Penguin Random House LLC

Text copyright © 2016 by GDL Foods, Inc. Illustrations copyright © 2016 by Francesca Gambatesa. All rights reserved. Published by Grosset & Dunlap, an imprint of Penguin Random House LLC, 345 Hudson Street, New York, New York 10014. GROSSET & DUNLAP is a trademark of Penguin Random House LLC. Printed in the USA.

Library of Congress Cataloging-in-Publication Data is available.

ISBN 978-0-448-48395-5 (pbk)   10 9 8 7 6 5 4 3 2

ISBN 978-0-448-48396-2 (hc)   10 9 8 7 6 5 4 3 2 1

Chapter 1

Alfie sighed and pulled at a loose string on his bedspread.
His sister, Emilia, sat next to him with her arms crossed.
She sighed, too. Their great-aunt Zia Donatella laughed.

"Such *facce tristi*," Zia said in Italian. "Such sad faces!"

"Do you really have to go?" Alfie asked as Zia packed
her suitcase.

"Yeah," Emilia added. "Can't you stay just a little bit
longer?"

Zia smiled and sat down beside them on Alfie's
bed. "I'm meeting friends in Oslo in a few days. I can't
disappoint them, either!"

"That's in Norway, right?" Emilia asked.

"Yes!" Alfie answered before Zia had a chance. "It's the capital of Norway."

Alfie and Emilia had known for a while that Zia's stay with the Bertolizzi family was coming to an end, but it didn't make her leaving any easier. After all, Zia had traveled the world a few times over. She'd visited places as far and wide as Morocco, Russia, and Argentina!

Staying with Alfie, Emilia, and their parents was probably the longest Zia had lived in one place in quite a while.

Alfie looked at all the maps that hung on the walls of his bedroom. Having Zia around and hearing her travel stories made Alfie love geography even more. He also realized how little time he'd actually spent in his room since Zia had been their guest.

"Won't it be nice to have your bedroom back?" Zia asked, as if reading his mind.

Alfie shrugged. "It will. But I'd be happy to let you keep it if it meant you were staying longer." He'd grown used to the lumpy pullout sofa in the office. It didn't really bother him anymore.

"Or you could stay in my room for a while!" Emilia jumped in. "I wouldn't mind."

Alfie raised an eyebrow. Now that Emilia was thirteen, she spent more time in her bedroom than ever. It was hard for Alfie to imagine her giving that up.

Zia laughed again and touched the brightly colored stone necklace she always wore. "You're both very sweet. Maybe next time I'll stay in your room, Emilia."

Alfie perked up at the thought of Zia being their guest again. He got up and walked over to the big world map tacked to his wall. He looked at all the places they'd visited since Zia came to stay: Naples, Italy; Paris, France; Hong Kong, China; Rio de Janeiro, Brazil; and New Orleans, Maui, and Miami in the United States.

Alfie turned to Emilia and grinned. "Look at all the places we've gone!"

Emilia jumped up and joined him at the map. "We've actually been around the world."

Not only was Zia a first-class world traveler herself, but she had turned Alfie and Emilia into seasoned travelers as well—all thanks to a little magic.

Zia rolled up a pair of jeans and placed them in her almost-full suitcase. "I don't know what you two are talking about," she said with a smile. "But I do know that *someone* will be twelve in a couple of days!"

Alfie beamed. He couldn't wait for his birthday. And he was so glad Zia would still be there to celebrate with them. "That's right," he said. "You know what would be a great birthday present, Zia?"

"What, *ragazzo*?"

"You staying with us longer!" Alfie replied.

"Yes!" Emilia chimed in.

Zia smiled, closed her suitcase, and zipped up the side. "Come on," she said. "Let's go make a snack. Good food makes everything better."

Alfie and Emilia had a hard time arguing with that. They raced out of the room and followed Zia down to the kitchen.

Chapter 2

The next morning at breakfast, Alfie walked into the
kitchen and found his parents rushing around as usual.
Emilia sat at the table eating her scrambled eggs with
her head stuck in a history book. Emilia was passionate
about history in the same way that Alfie loved geography.
Alfie poured himself a glass of orange juice and took a
seat next to Emilia.

Just then, Zia breezed into the room. She stopped
short and looked at Mom and Dad. "You two look
exhausted!" she said.

Alfie looked up and saw that Mom's shirt was
wrinkled on one side, and Dad was yawning. Zia was

right: They looked frazzled, tired, and worn-out.

"Big project at work," Mom said, taking a bite of toast while she tried to smooth out her shirt. "I was up half the night."

"And I've got a very important meeting first thing this morning," Dad added. "Clients are flying in from New York."

Zia sighed. "You both really need a break. You've been working nonstop for months!"

"Yeah, Mom and Dad," Emilia agreed, looking up from her book. "We've barely even seen you."

Alfie nodded. Mom and Dad were always busy, but lately it had reached a crazy point.

Dad kissed Emilia on top of her head. "We'll be home for dinner tonight. I promise."

"Yes, we'll see you tonight!" Mom said with a tired smile.

Alfie was about to bring up plans for his birthday party when Dad ruffled Alfie's hair and grabbed his briefcase. "See you tonight, champ!" he said as he headed for the garage.

Mom trailed right behind, balancing her bag and travel coffee mug. "Have a good day!" she called back.

Alfie, Emilia, and Zia stared at one another. It felt like a tornado had just blown through the kitchen.

"What are we going to do?" Alfie asked.

"I don't know." Emilia shook her head. "They barely even sleep anymore. It's crazy!"

Zia poured herself a cup of coffee. "I have an idea," she said. "We'll make a special dinner tonight and talk to them about finally starting to plan that family trip they've been dreaming about. I think if the three of us band together, we might be able to convince them."

"Good idea!" Alfie said. "We've been talking about that for ages."

Emilia nodded. "I guess I stopped thinking about it since Alfie and I have traveled so much on our own lately. But you're right, it's definitely time!"

Alfie laughed. "Where should we go with Mom and Dad?"

"Norway sounds interesting," Emilia joked. "Mind if we tag along on your trip, Zia?"

Zia laughed.

"Do you like visiting Norway?" Emilia asked.

"Believe it or not," Zia said, "this will actually be my first time going. I'm really looking forward to it, and I'll let you know all the details."

"How about some place in the United States, like San Francisco?" Alfie chimed in. "Didn't you say you've always wanted to visit there, too?"

"Yes, I have! And I know your parents would like that. There are plenty of cities in the United States they still haven't visited."

"We could take a ferry to Alcatraz and ride the cable cars!" Emilia said.

"And eat burritos!" Alfie added.

"Or what about Boston?" Emilia said. "There's so much history there. The American Revolution, the Boston Tea Party, Paul Revere's house . . ."

"Boston definitely has plenty of history!" Zia agreed.

Alfie flopped back in his chair. "There are so many

cool places. How are we supposed to choose just one?"

Zia laughed as she put away the breakfast dishes. Alfie and Emilia stood up to help. "We'll talk more about it tonight," Zia said. "In the meantime, you two should brush your teeth and get ready for school. I don't want you to be late!"

"Okay," Alfie and Emilia replied. They hurried to get ready for their day, but Alfie couldn't stop thinking about where they might go. There was Seattle, New York City, Chicago . . . and that was just in the United States! It was exciting to think about a new trip as a family. He just hoped Mom and Dad could finally stop working long enough to plan something.

Chapter 3

Alfie and Emilia went straight to the kitchen when they got home from school, following the telltale sounds and smells of Zia preparing a meal. Ingredients were spread all over the counter: fresh spinach, broccoli, mushrooms, and tomatoes. A pot of water was boiling on the stove.

"*Ciao, bambini!* How was practice?"

"It was good," Alfie and Emilia replied together. Alfie had band practice while Emilia had dance team.

"We went over my solo for the end-of-the-year concert," Alfie said proudly. "We're working on a new song that's kind of hard, but I really like it."

"That's fantastic," Zia responded. "Are you going to

play this song with your other band, too?"

"I hope so!" Alfie smiled. Since he had done such a great job in the spring concert, Alfie's band teacher, Mr. Erikson, asked him to join a special school band. They'd already performed at the mall, a senior center, and even an animal shelter adoption event.

"And what about you?" Zia asked Emilia. "How was dance?"

"Great!" Emilia said as she popped a tomato slice into her mouth. "I've been teaching the other girls on my squad some of the salsa moves I learned in Miami. It's been so fun!"

"*Ben fatto!* Well done," Zia said.

"What are we making for dinner?" Alfie asked.

"I thought we'd make a veggie lasagna tonight."

Alfie's stomach rumbled at the thought of it. "Yes!" he cheered. "What can we do to help?"

"I think I've got the lasagna under control. Why don't you two work on a salad and some garlic bread?"

"Sounds good!" Emilia said as she pulled a big salad bowl out from under the counter.

They talked as they worked and cleaned up along the way. After all the cooking they'd done together, Alfie, Emilia, and Zia had become an all-star team in the kitchen. Before long, Zia was pulling the bubbling, delicious lasagna from the oven. Emilia put the toasted garlic bread in a basket, and Alfie made a dressing for the salad.

"Oh, that smells delicious!" Mom said, coming in from the garage.

"It sure does," Dad added. "I'm starving!"

They set their briefcases in the hall and joined Alfie, Emilia, and Zia at the dining-room table.

"Thank you so much for making this," Mom said. "It looks like it was a lot of work."

"Zia did most of it," Alfie said.

"Nonsense!" Zia replied. "It was absolutely a team effort."

Everybody took a seat at the table and began to dig into the meal.

"How was work?" Emilia asked.

"Oh, it was fine," Mom said, waving her hand. "But let's not talk about work anymore today. I want to hear where Zia is planning to go on her travels."

Zia smiled. "Well, the first stop—right after Alfie's birthday party, of course—is Norway. And then it's on to Sweden and Denmark. I'm meeting a chef in Copenhagen who's doing some really innovative things there with local ingredients."

"That sounds fantastic," Dad said, blowing on a forkful of lasagna before popping it into his mouth.

"What about after that, Zia?" Alfie asked. "Will you come back here?"

Zia laughed and squeezed Alfie's arm. "Not right away. I haven't made any firm plans after Copenhagen yet, but it's been a while since I've visited Naples, and my friends there are begging me to come for the *Festa di Pizza*."

"Hey! That's where we—" Alfie started before noticing the curious looks from Mom and Dad. "I mean . . . we talked about that last year."

"That's right," Zia said, hiding a smile. "We did talk about the *Festa di Pizza* when I first came to stay."

"Well, that sounds like a wonderful idea," Mom said. "I haven't been to the *Festa di Pizza* since I was a little girl. Oh, kids, you really should see it—and taste it! Naples has the best pizza in the world!"

Alfie and Emilia smiled and nodded knowingly. Zia gave them a sly wink.

"So, Alfie," Dad jumped in. "You still haven't told us what you want for your birthday."

Alfie scooped a big hunk of garlic bread into his mouth and shrugged. He chewed quickly. "I guess I haven't figured it out yet."

"Well, you'd better think hard. It's almost time for your party!" Mom said.

"I'll keep you posted!" Alfie joked.

After the last of the lasagna had been eaten, Zia stood up from the table and began to clear away the dishes. Mom and Dad started to stand, too. "No, no." Zia put her hand out. "You just relax."

"We'll help, Zia," Emilia said.

"Yeah," Alfie agreed, standing up and grabbing the empty salad bowl.

"Thank you," Dad said. "What a nice surprise this dinner was."

As Alfie and Emilia cleared the plates and filled the dishwasher, Zia began to busy herself by pulling new ingredients from the cupboards. She put six eggs, butter, flour, sugar, baking powder, and a small bottle of anise extract on the counter.

"Don't tell me you're cooking something else, Donatella?" Dad looked at Zia with wide eyes.

"I still haven't made my famous *pizzelles* since I've been here. I thought they would be a nice treat tonight."

"Oh, *pizzelles*!" Mom's face lit up. "We haven't had those in ages!"

"What are they?" Alfie asked.

"They are traditional Italian waffle cookies," Zia said.

"In Italy we used to make them at Christmastime, for birthdays, for weddings . . . for all special occasions, really," Mom added, excitement rising in her voice.

"Arianna, where do you keep your iron?" Zia asked Mom.

"It's in the laundry room," Alfie chimed in.

Zia and Mom laughed. "Not that iron," Mom said, getting up from the table. She walked over to the cupboard above the fridge and stood on her tiptoes to reach inside. She pulled out something that looked like a small waffle iron. "This is a *pizzelle* iron." Mom lifted the handle and showed Alfie and Emilia the inside. There were four small circles, two on the handle side and two on the base. One side had a waffle pattern and the other had a pattern that looked like a flower or a snowflake.

"Cool!" Alfie said.

Zia placed some butter in a pan on the stovetop. As it melted, she started cracking eggs into a mixing bowl.

"I want to help!" Emilia said.

"Me too!" Alfie added.

Dad stood up from the table. "Let's all help!" he said.

"Bene! How nice!" Zia smiled. "Emilia, you finish adding the eggs and beat them together. Alfie, measure out one and a half cups of sugar. When Emilia's eggs are beaten, you can slowly add the sugar as she stirs."

"Mauricio and I will sift together the flour and the baking powder," Mom said. "How many cups of flour, Zia?"

"Three and a half cups of flour and four teaspoons of baking powder, please," Zia replied.

Once the eggs and sugar were mixed together, Zia took the butter off the stovetop to let it cool. Then she slowly added it to the mixture along with two tablespoons of the anise extract.

"What does anise taste like?" Emilia asked.

"It has a little bit of a licorice-type flavor," Zia replied.

"Mmmmm," Alfie said. He loved licorice!

Next, Mom and Dad mixed the sifted flour and baking powder with the rest of the ingredients while Zia plugged in the iron.

"Now we drop tablespoon-size balls of dough onto the center of the iron," Zia said. "You can grab the dough with your hands if you want to."

Alfie dug right into the bowl of dough. When he pulled out his hand, it was covered with the sticky mixture. He held his hand in the air. "It looks like I'm wearing a baseball mitt," he said.

Everybody laughed. "A baseball mitt made of cookie dough!" Emilia said.

Alfie scraped most of the dough back into the bowl and rolled the rest into a small ball in his palm.

"Perfect," Zia said. "Now carefully place it in the center of the iron."

"Yes, *stai attento*—be careful, Alfie," Mom added. "The iron gets very hot."

Alfie set his ball of dough onto the iron. Then Zia closed it and looked at the clock. "It only needs about thirty seconds to bake."

"Wow!" Alfie said. "That's fast."

Mom got a cooling rack from under the stove and put it on the counter. "The *pizzelles* can cool on this."

Zia lifted the iron lid and peeked inside. The *pizzelle* was golden-brown with the beautiful snowflake pattern etched into it.

"They're such pretty cookies!" Emilia said. "I can't wait to try one!"

Alfie totally agreed with his sister. It took some serious willpower not to reach out and grab the first *pizzelle* from the iron!

One by one, the family continued making the Italian *pizzelles* together.

"I think the best *pizzelles* I've ever had actually came from a small bakery in South Philadelphia," Zia said as she put away the rest of the cookie ingredients. "Well, aside from the ones we make, of course."

"Have you been to Philadelphia, Mom and Dad?" Alfie asked.

"No, never," Dad said.

"We tried to go once, before the kids were born. Remember, Mauricio?" Mom asked. "But there was that huge snowstorm and all the airports were shut down."

"I remember," Dad said. "And we talked several times about going back and just never did. I've always wanted to visit."

"Me too," Emilia said. "Philadelphia has *so* much history! The Declaration of Independence was signed there, and the Constitution was written and signed there, too."

"And the Liberty Bell is there," Alfie added.

"That's right," Mom said. "When did you visit Philadelphia, Zia?"

"It was a few years back," Zia replied. "I visited some Italian friends who moved there quite some time ago. Historically, there has always been a big population of Italians in Philadelphia."

"Did you like it there?" Emilia asked.

"Very much!" Zia said. "The people are so friendly. It

is called the City of Brotherly Love, after all."

"Maybe we should go to Philadelphia on our family vacation," Alfie suggested.

"I think that's a great idea," Dad said.

"Let's put it on the list!" Mom said as she finished wiping down the countertop.

"I think we're ready for some *pizzelles*," Zia said. She piled a bunch of the thin, wafer-like cookies onto a plate and took them over to the dining-room table. Alfie followed with a stack of napkins. He couldn't wait to try this new Italian treat!

"Zia, Alfie, and I were talking this morning, and we were wondering if we could start planning our family trip," Emilia said as they sat down at the table.

"Yes, yes," Mom said casually. "We will do that soon."

"But when?" Alfie pushed.

"Once things at the office die down a little bit," Dad said. "Like Mom said, we'll do it soon."

Alfie and Emilia exchanged a frustrated look. Zia gave

them a small, encouraging smile.

"Well, dig in, everybody," Zia said.

They each took a cookie from the plate. Alfie
inhaled the subtle scent of
the anise. He took
a bite, enjoying
the slightly crispy,
slightly chewy
texture of the waffle

cookie. "Yum!" he said. "It's sweet and buttery."

Everyone nodded in unison, too busy chewing to talk.

"So good," Dad finally said. "Reminds me of being a
kid back home." He closed his eyes as he took another
bite.

Alfie closed his eyes, too, to savor the rest of his
cookie. For a split second, just as he started to get that
familiar dip and flutter in his stomach, he thought maybe
the *pizzelles* were going to transport them back to Naples.
But he was wrong!

Chapter 4

When Alfie opened his eyes, he was on a city sidewalk. But it wasn't a tight, narrow sidewalk lining a cobblestone street like he'd seen in Naples. It was a redbrick sidewalk with old brick buildings and trees on either side. A couple walked past, speaking English. Emilia stood next to Alfie and touched his arm. Alfie knew she was also trying to figure out where they might be.

"Where are we?" Alfie heard behind him.

"What happened?" another voice added.

Alfie and Emilia whirled around to find their parents and Zia standing on the sidewalk behind them!

"You're here!" Alfie cried.

"You came with us!" Emilia added. "Thank you, Zia!"

Neither of them could believe it. And by the looks on Mom's and Dad's faces, they couldn't, either!

Zia smiled wide. "I thought it would be a fun surprise for Alfie's birthday. One last adventure before I go—for the whole family."

"This is the best surprise ever!" Alfie said, hugging Zia around the waist.

Mom held out her hands. "I don't understand what's going on!"

"Are we in Philadelphia, Zia?" Emilia asked.

"Yes, we are."

"Yay!" Emilia cheered. "I'm so excited!"

"But how did we get here?" Dad asked, turning in a circle and staring up at the buildings surrounding them.

"Magic!" Alfie and Emilia cried together. "Zia's magic."

"Magic?" Mom and Dad repeated.

"Zia has sent us on a bunch of adventures using the magic in her cooking. But this is the first time we've all gone together!"

With Zia's help, Alfie and Emilia quickly filled their parents in on some of the places they'd visited thanks to their great-aunt's recipes.

Mom's mouth dropped open. "I always knew your cooking was special, Zia, but I didn't know it was *this* special!"

"Well, now you know," Zia replied. "So let's have a little family adventure in Philadelphia, shall we?"

Mom gave Zia a quick hug.

"Y-yes. Okay, sure!" Dad said, still getting his bearings.

"But where will we stay?" Mom asked, worry entering her voice. "What will we do?"

"Leave that to us," Alfie said, motioning to Emilia and Zia.

"That's right," Emilia said. "We'll take care of everything!"

Mom's face started to soften. "You're so grown-up all of a sudden!"

And with that, they started down the sidewalk, taking in the heart of historic Philadelphia surrounding them.

Alfie squinted up at the afternoon sun. It felt strong and warm for late spring—like summer was just around the corner. They walked down the peaceful brick street. The sidewalks were clean with big trees planted all along the way. Some of the redbrick buildings had wide windows with small square windowpanes. They looked like they might have been old factory buildings at one point, but now some were apartments and others were small shops. Alfie liked the feel of the quiet old neighborhood. After a few blocks, they ducked down another narrow side street and continued on for a bit before stopping to look around. That's when Alfie noticed the sign behind him: THE LIBERTY HOTEL. "Why don't we stay here?" he asked, gesturing to the gold plaque on the redbrick building.

"The Liberty Hotel," Zia repeated. "That sounds familiar for some reason . . . Let's take a look."

They entered the small lobby of the building and looked around. Old marble floors lined the space, with a few big plants in ceramic planters against the walls. A worn velvet couch sat off to one side, and a large polished wood desk stood in front of them. There was a sign on the desk that read "Welcome to the historic Liberty Hotel. This building was constructed in 1826."

"Emilia, look," Alfie said, pointing to the sign.

Emilia read the sign and smiled. "Whoa! That's the same year Thomas Jefferson and John Adams died. They both died within hours of each other on the Fourth of July."

"How weird," Alfie said, looking around the room.

"I have been here before!" Zia suddenly exclaimed. "I knew it was familiar. My friends brought me here for dinner. This is a very well-known historic hotel in Philly."

Dad tapped the bell on top of the desk. A minute later,

a man appeared from another room. "Good afternoon!" he said. He had a warm, friendly smile and looked to be around Alfie and Emilia's dad's age. "Welcome to the Liberty Hotel. I'm John."

"Hi, John," Mom said. "I'm Arianna Bertolizzi. This is my aunt Donatella, my husband, Mauricio, and our kids, Alfredo and Emilia."

Alfie bristled a little bit at the use of his full name, but he waved and smiled all the same.

"Nice to meet you all!" John said. "What can I do for you?"

"Do you have any rooms available?" Zia asked.

"Absolutely," John replied. "How many would you like?"

"Three rooms would be ideal," Dad said.

John nodded and opened a book on the desk in front of him. "We can put you on our Constitution floor. We have a single room and then two double rooms with an interior door that connects them."

"That's perfect," Mom said.

"Great," said John, writing the Bertolizzis' names in his book. "My family and I run the hotel, so you'll meet my daughter and my wife during your stay. We serve breakfast, lunch, and dinner in the hotel restaurant, and if there's anything at all that you need, please let me know!"

"Thank you so much," Dad said, handing John his credit card. He turned to Zia and whispered, "Good thing my wallet was in my pocket!"

"I've got money, too," Alfie chimed in. "I always carry my allowance money with me now, just in case." He grinned at Zia.

Mom and Dad laughed. "That's smart thinking, son," Dad said.

John held out three keys. "You're on the third floor. The elevator is just over there, to the left of the plants.

Can I help you with any luggage?" he asked, scanning the space around them.

"Oh...," Mom said.

Alfie could tell she didn't know what to say, so he jumped in. "Our bags are in the car. We'll get them later."

Mom and Dad gave Alfie a look. Maybe his fib came a little too easily!

"Okay, great," John said. "Enjoy your stay. And again, if there's anything you need, please let us know."

They walked over to the elevator. It was an old wooden model with a metal grate that creaked as it opened. They squeezed into the small space, and Dad closed the metal grate behind them before pulling the lever for the third floor. The elevator paused for a moment before it moaned and groaned and began a very slow climb to their floor. Alfie could see the floors pass by through the grate as the elevator made its way upward. He was a little unsure whether they would actually make it, but a minute later they were stepping out.

"Whew!" Mom said. "Maybe we'll take the stairs from now on."

"No way!" Alfie said. "That was so cool! It must be the original elevator."

"Elevators weren't invented until the 1850s, so they must have put this in later," his sister corrected him. She smiled at her brother. "But it's still really neat."

"Still crazy!" Alfie replied.

Dad led the way down the hall. He handed Zia her key and then unlocked the other two doors. Alfie and Emilia walked into their room. Alfie thought it looked a little worn, and he could see some paint peeling near the ceiling. "It's not as nice as the suite we stayed in when we were in Maui," he said to Emilia.

"That *was* pretty nice," Emilia said with a giggle. She walked over and smelled the fresh flowers in a vase on the nightstand. "But I like it here. This building has much more character."

Alfie noticed a framed child's drawing on the wall.

Emilia was right. Despite looking a little rough around the edges, this hotel had a cozy, comfortable feeling—like staying at a friend's house. And it had a nice view. He could see between several buildings to one of the rivers in the distance.

Alfie and Emilia went into Mom and Dad's room. Zia joined them from her room. "What a quaint hotel!" she said.

Mom nodded. "It's very comfortable." She sat down on the edge of the bed. "And it's good that it's the weekend—although I did tell my boss I'd be in for a few hours tomorrow. I guess I'll just give her a call..."

"Don't worry!" Alfie said. "Whenever we get home, it's like not a minute has passed since we left."

Mom's and Dad's eyes widened.

"Wow," Mom breathed, looking a little in shock. "I just... I don't know what to think!"

Zia sat down next to Mom and patted her hand. "It's all perfectly safe, Arianna. I promise."

"But how does it work?" Mom asked.

"A chef never reveals her secrets. You should know that by now!" Zia said with a wink. Mom smiled. "And Alfie's right," Zia continued. "When we return home, it will be the same time that it was when we left."

"We don't know how she does it," Alfie said with a laugh.

"Yeah," Emilia added. "She's never even really admitted it before!"

Dad wrinkled his brow, like he was trying to figure it all out. But then he stood up and grinned. "Well, then, let's go see what Philly has in store for us, shall we?"

"Yes!" Alfie and Emilia cheered.

Chapter 5

The Bertolizzi family found the staircase and took it back down to the lobby. Alfie liked the worn, creaky, carpet-covered steps and the smooth wooden banister. He imagined all the people who had climbed these stairs since 1826! He knew Emilia was thinking the same thing. She walked slowly, taking in every detail.

Down in the sunny lobby, they headed for the front door of the hotel.

"Hello!" a voice said from behind them.

Alfie and Emilia turned first to see a girl about their age standing behind the reception desk. She had long shiny brown hair and a big friendly smile that matched her dad's.

"I'm Emma," she said. "My dad told me that you just checked in."

"Hi." Emilia stepped forward. "I'm Emilia. This is my brother, Alfie, our parents, and our great-aunt Donatella."

Alfie was relieved Emilia didn't use his full name this time.

"Nice to meet you!" Emma said. "Welcome to our hotel."

"We're very happy to be here!" Mom said. "How old are you, Emma?"

"I'm eleven and three-quarters," Emma replied.

"Me too!" Alfie said. "Well, actually, my birthday is in a couple of days, so I guess I'm almost twelve."

"Happy almost birthday!" Emma said. "Where are you off to?"

"We're not actually sure," Emilia answered. "We were just going to explore the city, but we don't know much about it."

"Do you need a tour guide?" Emma asked. "I'd be

happy to take you to some of the sites. I love showing our guests around!"

"That would be wonderful, Emma. Thank you," Zia said.

Emma's face lit up even more. "Great! I'll just let my parents know."

Emma dashed into the back room and returned a minute later with a small purse slung across her body. "All set. Let's go!"

Emma led the way out of the hotel and over to a busy main street in the opposite direction of where the family had arrived. "Our hotel is in the middle of a historic district called Old City," she explained. "The Liberty Bell and Independence Hall are basically right around the corner."

"Wow," Emilia sighed. "I can't imagine living this close to so much history."

Emma flashed a smile. "It's pretty cool."

They walked a few blocks, enjoying the sun and the

mix of older brick buildings like they'd seen earlier and newer glass-and-steel structures. Before long, they came upon a square with a couple of large buildings that were a mix of the two—redbrick and lots of glass. It was the Liberty Bell Center.

"I'm so excited!" Emilia said, jumping in place.

"Philadelphia was made for you!" Alfie laughed. "In case you hadn't noticed, Emilia *loves* history," Alfie explained to Emma.

Emma laughed, too. "Looks like it!"

Emma led the family into the building. They toured the center, taking in all the pictures, illustrations, and videos of the bell throughout the years. There were photos of Civil War generals, abolitionists, and civil rights leaders who used the bell as a symbol for liberty.

After that, they walked into the big glass room where the bell was displayed. Inscribed around the top it read: "PROCLAIM LIBERTY THROUGHOUT ALL THE LAND UNTO ALL THE INHABITANTS THEREOF."

"It's huge!" Dad said. "I didn't realize it was so big."

Mom pointed to a sign. "It says here that the bell weighs two thousand pounds and is twelve feet in circumference."

"That's one big bell," Dad said.

"There are two cracks in it!" Alfie whispered, pointing to the massive bell.

Emilia nodded vigorously. "I just read about this in history class! When the first crack happened, the repair workers actually widened it with rivets to try to keep it from spreading. But then a second smaller crack appeared, and the bell couldn't be rung anymore."

"Wow," Alfie said. "All that work for a bell they couldn't use."

"The bell used to hang in Independence Hall across the street when it was the Pennsylvania State House," Emma said. "We can go there next."

"Great!" Emilia said. Alfie smiled at his sister.

They entered Independence Hall just in time for the next guided tour. The family quickly got in line and followed the guide through all the rooms and halls.

"It took workers twenty-one years to build this entire hall," the guide said as he led them down a corridor. "They worked on it as money became available.

It was finally completed in 1753."

"I had no idea!" Emilia whispered to Emma.

"Yeah," Emma whispered back. "It's really cool! The Declaration of Independence and the Constitution were both signed here. And it was even used as a hospital for wounded soldiers in the Revolutionary War."

"Wow," the tour guide said, overhearing Emma. "You have quite a future as a tour guide!" Alfie thought he saw Emma blush as the whole tour turned and smiled.

Once the tour was over, Emma and the Bertolizzis walked out into the square.

"That was *so* cool!" Emilia said.

"It really was," Mom agreed.

"All that history made me hungry!" Alfie said.

Everybody laughed.

"I know just the place," Emma said, leading the family up to bustling Market Street.

After walking several blocks, they reached a brick building with a big sign in red letters above the entrance.

"Reading Terminal Market," Alfie read aloud.

"This is one of the oldest markets in America," Emma told them. "It opened in 1892."

"Wow!" Emilia said.

They stepped inside the busy space. There were signs everywhere pointing to different types of vendors: meat shops, cheese shops, bakeries, produce, coffee, ice cream—almost anything you could think of!

"There are also stalls that sell books, flowers, and lots of other things!" Emma said.

The family walked the aisles of the market, accepting samples of delicious breads, cheeses, and prepared foods. Mom and Zia stopped to look at a stand full of cookbooks. While they were doing that, Emma walked over to a ceramics stall and spoke to the woman there.

"I'll have your new vases ready next week," the woman told Emma. "I think they're going to be the perfect centerpieces for your tables at the restaurant."

"I'll let my mom know," Emma said. "We're working

on sprucing up the restaurant, so I know she's really excited to see them."

"Tell your parents hello for me," the woman added. "I'll be sure to call as soon as they're finished."

Emma nodded and waved good-bye. Then she led the way down the aisle to a pretzel counter at the end of the row.

"Soft pretzels are big here in Philly," Emma said. "I thought you might like to try one."

"Yes, please!" Alfie said.

They all ordered salted pretzels and then chose different dipping sauces. Alfie and Emma had cheese sauce on theirs, while  Emilia tried honey mustard. Zia and Dad both went for spicy mustard, and Mom chose regular yellow mustard. They washed down the pretzels with frozen lemonade. Alfie was in heaven dipping his warm, doughy pretzel into the cheese sauce.

Mom, Dad, and Zia sat on a bench next to the pretzel

stand while Alfie, Emilia, and Emma stood at a tall counter.

"How long has your family owned the Liberty Hotel?" Emilia asked Emma between bites.

"It's been passed down through my dad's family for at least fifty years," Emma said. "And it's been a hotel since the early nineteen hundreds. Before that, it was a hospital. My parents moved in when they first got married and took over from my grandparents, so they've lived there since before I was born! My mom makes all the food in the restaurant from scratch. She taught herself to cook, and now she's teaching me."

"Zia has been teaching Alfie and me to cook, too," Emilia said. "It's so much fun."

Emma nodded. "I think I might want to be a chef someday. Well, either that or a writer . . . Or a musician . . ." Emma laughed. "I guess I haven't really decided yet."

"I've thought about being a chef, too, thanks to Zia,"

Alfie said. "But I also like music a lot. I play the drums!"

Emma beamed. "I'm going to learn guitar this summer. I can't wait!"

"Nice!" Alfie said.

"I can't imagine living in a hotel—especially such an old one," Emilia said. "It must be so cool!"

"It is! I really love it," Emma answered. "We have an apartment on the top floor, but whenever I have friends over to spend the night, my parents let us choose one of the rooms to stay in."

"That would be *so* awesome!" Alfie said.

"For my birthday last year, they let us have an entire floor to ourselves!"

"That's what I want for my next birthday!" Emilia said.

"Good luck convincing Mom and Dad," Alfie replied.

"Living in a hotel has its downsides, too, though," Emma said, suddenly growing serious. "At least living in our hotel . . ."

"What do you m—" Alfie started to ask.

"Ready to go?" Dad interrupted, approaching the counter.

Everybody was up and moving before Alfie had a chance to ask Emma what she'd meant. He'd have to remember to ask her later. He wanted to know what could possibly be bad about living in a hotel!

Chapter 6

Twenty minutes later, the family and Emma walked into the hotel lobby happily talking about all the cool stuff they'd seen and learned that day. But they stopped short in front of the reception desk. There was a group of angry guests, surrounded by their luggage. One man had his arms folded across his chest with a scowl on his face. Another woman stood off to the side, tapping her foot.

Emma's dad, John, was behind the desk, shuffling paperwork and looking frazzled.

"Normally we charge a fee for a last-minute cancellation," John was saying. "But we will waive the fee this time."

"Good," the woman said. "I'm happy to pay for the nights that we stayed, but I don't want to be charged anything extra."

Emma walked behind the desk and stood next to her dad. "Is everything all right?" she asked.

John put on a tense smile. "These guests were unhappy with their stay, unfortunately, so they're checking out early."

"Oh," Emma said as she looked at her dad.

"There was a leaking pipe in my room," the man complained. "Water was everywhere! We were so excited to stay at the famous Liberty Hotel, but it just didn't live up to our expectations."

Emma's dad finished refunding the unhappy guests' credit cards. Then he helped them carry their luggage out to their cars. When he returned, he tried to put a smile on his face, but it seemed forced. "Sorry about that, folks," he said. "We've been having this problem for a while. Has your stay been uncomfortable?"

"Not at all," Mom said.

"I think the rooms are very charming," Zia added. "I was so happy when we found your hotel!"

John nodded. "I've been keeping up with repairs as much as I can, but lately it's just one thing after another—

as soon as one thing is fixed, something else breaks."

Alfie realized this must be what Emma meant about living in the hotel having its downsides.

"That's a tough situation," Dad said.

"We have the option to sell," John continued. "But I hope it doesn't come to that."

Emma turned to Alfie and Emilia. "I hate the idea of selling," she told them. "Especially to a developer."

"A developer?" Emilia asked.

"Yeah. He's known all over town for tearing down old buildings and putting up new condos," she continued.

Emilia gasped. "He wouldn't really tear down the Liberty Hotel, would he?"

Emma frowned. "He might," she said.

"That would be terrible!" Emilia cried. "What would your family do if you sold?"

"My grandma has a house in South Philly with plenty of room," Emma replied. "She's already said we can live there as long as we want if we have to sell the hotel.

It's just so hard to imagine not having it in our family anymore." Emma sighed. "I'm sorry to be so down. Everything will work out... somehow."

"It will!" Emilia tried to sound encouraging.

Alfie nodded, but he still didn't know what to say.

After a moment, Emma finally spoke. "I should go help my mom in the kitchen," she said. "See you later."

"Thanks for everything today," Alfie said. "It was really awesome having our very own tour guide."

"You're welcome," Emma said with a smile.

The family made their way up to the third floor. Alfie and Emilia lagged behind.

"*Will* everything work out?" Alfie asked Emilia.

Emilia frowned. "I don't know. I hope so!"

"I wish there was something we could do to help," Alfie said.

"Me too," Emilia replied.

Chapter 7

After a rest at the hotel, the family was hungry and ready for dinner! They headed downstairs and found John at the reception desk.

"Do you have any recommendations for dinner?" Mom asked him.

"Well, there's our restaurant here at the Liberty. Or I'm happy to recommend something else if there's a specific type of food you're looking for."

"Oh, let's eat here!" Zia said. "My friends brought me here years ago, and I'd love to try it again."

John beamed. "My wife will be thrilled. Follow me!"

John led the way into the restaurant. There were

groups of diners at several other tables. Alfie scanned the food as they walked past. It looked really good.

They sat at a large round table in the corner of the restaurant. Before long, Emma came out of the kitchen with a bunch of menus and a pitcher of water. "Hi! I'm so glad you came. We're doing a special seafood menu tonight," she said as she set the small handwritten menus on the table. "Normally our menu is more American food, but we're trying to spice things up and do a special menu a couple of nights a week."

"Everything looks delicious," Mom said as she looked at the menu.

"Yes, it does!" Zia agreed.

Emma filled their water glasses. "I'll be back to take your order."

"Thanks, Emma!" Emilia said.

Alfie looked at the menu. He saw clams, mussels, and scallops in one of the dishes. He pointed it out to Emilia. "Isn't this what was in that seafood paella in Miami?"

"Yes!" Emilia said. "I'm definitely getting that."

Alfie made a face. He definitely wasn't. Then his eyes landed on fish-and-chips. That sounded perfect.

Dad set his menu on the table. "I still can't believe you kids have been on so many adventures. Did you really have seafood paella in Miami?"

Alfie grinned. "Yep. At a food festival. We had lots of Cuban and other Caribbean food, too. It was so good!"

Mom looked at Zia and then back at Alfie and Emilia. "What else have you tried?"

"We went to the *Festa di Pizza* in Naples!" Alfie said. "And we tried frog legs in Paris."

Mom's and Dad's eyes grew wide. "You did?!"

"And we had chicken feet in Hong Kong, alligator tail in New Orleans, and poi in Hawaii!" Emilia added.

Emma approached their table again. "Are you ready to order?"

"I'll have the fish-and-chips, please!" Alfie said.

"And I'll have the seafood chowder," Emilia said.

"Great choices!" Emma said.

Mom ordered the halibut, Zia ordered crab cakes, and Dad ordered lobster tail. Mom gave him a look after Emma left. "Mauricio, that's the most expensive thing on the menu!"

"Hey! We're on vacation," Dad said. "Time to live it up!"

Everybody laughed, including Mom.

"I'm really amazed by the adventures you've had," Dad said. "What was your favorite part?"

"I think it's the people we've met," Emilia said. "Everyone was so friendly and happy to show us around."

"And it's already the same on this trip," Alfie added. "Emma and her family are such great hosts."

"They really are," Zia said, looking around the restaurant. "I feel so bad that they're having problems. It's such a great old building."

"I wonder what would happen to it if they had to sell," Mom said.

"That developer can't really tear it down, can he?" Emilia asked.

"Old buildings get replaced all the time," said Dad.

Before long, the busboy carried over a serving tray with steaming plates of hot seafood. Everyone dug in eagerly. Alfie dribbled a bit of malted vinegar over his fried fish and then dipped it in tartar sauce.

"Want a bite of my chowder?" Emilia asked Alfie. She had a sly look on her face, like she knew Alfie wouldn't like it.

That made him want to accept the challenge even more.

"Okay," he said, picking up a spoon. He made sure to get a bite that included a mussel. He let the rich broth coat his mouth with a burst of flavors. The mussel was a bit chewy, but it wasn't too bad this time. "It's still not my favorite, but I like the broth a lot."

Emilia nodded. "It's really delicious!"

"Mine is, too," Zia said. "The mango salsa on these crab cakes is such an interesting twist."

"I haven't had lobster tail in ages," Dad added between bites. "This makes it worth the wait."

Everyone dug in and enjoyed the delicious food. As the meal came to a close, Mom spoke up. "Alfie! Your birthday is in two days. You still haven't told us what you want!"

Alfie sat back from the table, full from his meal. "I've

been having so much fun in Philadelphia that I haven't really thought about it. I'm just not sure."

"Well, keep thinking," Dad said.

"I will."

"How was everything?" Emma asked as she and the busboy cleared away empty plates.

"It was wonderful," Zia said.

"I can't remember the last time I had seafood this good," Dad agreed.

Emma smiled proudly. "I'm so glad! Did you save room for dessert?"

Mom started to say no, but Dad chimed in. "What do you say, kids?"

"I've never said no to dessert before," Alfie answered immediately. "Why start now?"

Zia and Mom laughed. "I like your thinking," Zia said.

They decided to get two desserts to share: a Philadelphia cream cheese brownie and a piece of Dutch apple pie with vanilla ice cream.

Just as they finished the delicious desserts, a woman came out of the kitchen. "I'm Ann, Emma's mom," she said. "Emma has told me so much about you."

"It's really nice to meet you, Ann," Dad said. "You have such a beautiful hotel."

"Thank you!" Ann said.

"And your food is absolutely divine," Zia said. "Emma told us you're self-taught."

Ann laughed. "Yes, that's true. I've been cooking for a long time now. I have a few good tricks up my sleeve."

Zia smiled. "Perhaps we can trade some recipe secrets."

"That would be wonderful!" Ann said. "Why don't you join us for breakfast in the morning?"

"Thank you," Dad said. "We will!"

✳   ✳   ✳

After all that food, the Bertolizzis decided to take a walk.

As they walked out of the hotel and onto the quiet street, Alfie and Dad held their stomachs. Mom, Emilia, and Zia couldn't help but laugh.

"I knew you'd be too full, Mauricio," Mom said.

"I just couldn't help myself," Dad replied. "But walking will help me digest." The family strolled through the streets of Philadelphia. It was much quieter than it had been that afternoon, and a few places were closing for the night. Old-fashioned street lamps lit up the sidewalks and cast shadows on the brick buildings. Alfie thought the city looked even more historic at night than during the day.

On the corner of a busy street, they found a drugstore that was still open so they could buy toothpaste, toothbrushes, and a few other things. There were a couple of racks of touristy T-shirts, so they each picked out one of those. Emilia chose a shirt with a portrait of Ben Franklin. Alfie grabbed one with a picture of a cheesesteak.

"A cheesesteak?" Mom said, laughing. "Have you ever had one, Alfie?"

"Not yet!" Alfie answered. "But I bet I'll like it."

"I sure hope you do," Dad joked, poking Alfie in the stomach.

"We'll get a couple more things tomorrow when clothing stores are open," Mom said as she took their purchases to the counter.

✳   ✳   ✳

When they got back to the hotel, Mom convinced them to take the stairs up to their rooms. "We need all the exercise we can get after that meal!" she said.

"That food was so good," Alfie remarked. "They can't close the hotel!"

"I agree," Zia said. "I hope they can figure out a way to stay in business."

When they finally reached the third floor, everybody said good night and went to their rooms to settle in. Alfie and Emilia brushed their teeth and then jumped into the double beds.

"It's so different this time, having Mom and Dad and

Zia along," Emilia said as she turned off the lamp on her bedside table.

"I know!" Alfie agreed. "I like it, though—especially going to nice restaurants and ordering whatever we want!"

Emilia laughed. "That dinner was *so* yummy."

Just then, Alfie and Emilia heard a loud clanging noise.

"What was that?" Emilia said, quickly turning the lamp back on.

"I have no idea," Alfie replied. They heard the clang again.

"It . . . it must just be the old building, right?" Emilia asked tentatively.

"I hope so!" Alfie said. "Unless it's haunted, too."

Emilia threw a pillow at her brother. "Don't say that! I won't be able to sleep."

Alfie's laugh was interrupted by another loud noise. He wasn't sure he was going to be able to sleep, either!

Chapter 8

Alfie was awoken by a steady tapping noise. He slowly opened his eyes. What was that, anyway? Just then, Emilia got up from her bed and shuffled across the floor. She opened the door that connected the room to their parents' room. Alfie yawned loudly.

"Good morning!" Mom said in a singsong voice. "Time to get up!"

Alfie groaned and pulled up his covers. Emilia trudged back to her bed and sat on the edge, rubbing the sleep from her eyes.

Mom stepped into the room. "What's the matter with you two? I thought you'd be ready for another day of exploring before your dad and I were even awake!"

"I didn't sleep very well," Emilia said.

"Me either," Alfie mumbled through his bedsheet.

"Why not?" Mom asked.

Emilia shrugged. "The bed was comfortable, but there were so many loud noises!"

Mom nodded knowingly. "We heard some of that, too. It's just a very old building, and old buildings like to settle at night."

"It sounded more like the building was throwing a party than settling!" Alfie said.

Mom chuckled. "We're heading downstairs for breakfast with Zia. You two take a few minutes to wake up and get ready, then meet us down there."

"Okay," Emilia said through a yawn.

After a few minutes, Alfie and Emilia took the elevator down to the lobby and walked past the empty reception desk into the dining room of the restaurant. Mom, Dad, and Zia were seated at the same table they'd been at the night before. Emma and her mom stood talking to them, holding menus in their hands. There were four other tables of people aside from theirs. It looked like no one had eaten yet—the others were sipping coffee, tea, or juice.

"Good morning!" Emma said, a smile taking up her entire face.

"How did you sleep?" Ann asked.

Emilia and Alfie exchanged a quick glance. "Uh . . . good!" Emilia said. "Fine."

"Yeah," Alfie interjected. "We really love the view from our room!"

"I'm so glad," Ann said.

Emma handed them each a menu as they sat down. "What would you like to have?"

Alfie scanned the page and landed on exactly what he wanted. "I'll have banana pancakes, please!"

Emma beamed. "My mom just let me add those to the menu. They're my favorite! What about you, Emilia?"

Emilia took a minute to decide. "I think I'll have the spinach and feta omelet."

"Great!" Emma said, writing it on her small pad of paper.

"Did you order already?" Alfie asked his parents.

"We did," Dad responded. "Your mother and I are both having omelets, and Zia is having the frittata."

"What's a frittata?" Alfie asked.

Zia was about to answer when Emma chimed in. "It's like an open-faced omelet, or a quiche without the crust," she explained.

"That's right," Zia said. "I know I've made frittata for you before. It's Italian!"

"I remember!" Emilia said.

"Even the word is Italian," Mom added. "It comes from *friggere*, which means 'to fry.'"

"And fried always equals delicious," said Alfie.

The adults laughed and shook their heads.

"If it's not too much of an imposition, I'd love to see your kitchen," Zia told Ann.

"Absolutely!" Ann said. "Right this way."

"Great," Zia replied, setting down her menu and following Ann into the kitchen.

Emma smiled at the Bertolizzis and tucked her notepad into her apron. "I'm just going to take one more order, and then we'll get started on your food!"

"Thanks, Emma," Alfie said.

"Don't worry. We're not in a rush," Mom replied.

Alfie noticed how relaxed Mom seemed. He hadn't seen her look that way in a long time.

"What should we do today, kids?" Dad asked.

Alfie was about to respond when the lights went out. The whole dining room was plunged into darkness. Alfie could hear a few dishes and pots clanging in the kitchen. "What happened?"

"I guess the power went out," Dad said.

Not a minute later, John appeared from the front lobby, balancing a flashlight and an armload of matchbooks and candles. Dad jumped up to help him.

"I'm so sorry," John said, out of breath. "I can't think of the last time we had a power outage. I need to check the block and see if it's just our building."

Dad took the candles and books of matches from his hands. "You go take a look. I'll pass out the candles." Dad brought a couple of candles and a book of matches to each table and helped get them lit.

Ann came out of the kitchen carrying a flashlight. She asked Mom if she'd seen John and then hurried to find him. The family waited at their table, watching the candlelight flicker across the room. Emma and Zia walked out of the kitchen at the same time as Emma's parents returned from the lobby.

"I'm afraid the power is out in our entire building," John announced to all the guests. "It doesn't appear that any other buildings on the block have been affected. I just had the electrical checked in our mechanical room last week and nothing is off on the breaker switches or the fuse box."

There were murmurs and whispers among the other guests.

"I've called the power company and the electrician, and I'm sure the power will be restored shortly," John continued.

"We can serve pastries, fruit, and yogurt," Ann added. "But we won't be able to finish making your entrées. I'm so sorry for the inconvenience."

Now the murmurs among the guests were getting louder. One by one, the other tables started to get up and head out of the restaurant, candles in hand.

"I'm checking out," one woman said.

"Me too," said a man. "And I'm on the fourth floor. How am I going to get my luggage down if I can't use the elevator?"

"I'll help you, sir," John replied. His voice sounded tired and defeated.

Ann and Emma approached the Bertolizzis' table. They were the only ones still seated. "I'm so sorry about this," Ann said. "We just can't seem to catch a break. John has always been so on top of repairs and making sure the building is running smoothly. It's all so strange . . ."

"We understand," Zia said.

"I need to go help John," Ann continued. "I think some other guests are checking out early. But Emma can get you something to eat."

"We'll be just fine with some pastries and fruit. Not to worry," Mom said.

Emma rushed back to the kitchen and returned with a

plate of croissants and muffins and a big bowl of fruit.

"This looks great," Alfie said, helping himself to a blueberry muffin.

"I'm so sorry for everything," Emma said. Alfie could see her cheeks were flushed with embarrassment. "Can I take you out sightseeing again today?"

"We would love to have you as our tour guide again," Dad said, spearing a piece of pineapple with his fork.

"It's the least I can do," said Emma. "And it is one of my favorite things."

"It's settled then," Zia said.

Emma beamed. "I'll just finish up in the kitchen and meet you all in the lobby when you're done eating."

Alfie looked around the dark room. It was kind of fun to eat by candlelight. Though he did feel bad about all the problems Emma and her parents were having. He still hadn't figured out any way they could help them. He hoped he could think of something before it was time to go home!

Chapter 9

The Bertolizzis and Emma stepped out onto the sidewalk. "Now that I know you love history so much, I thought we could visit the Betsy Ross House today," Emma told them.

"Really?" Emilia squealed.

The family walked in the same direction as the Liberty Bell Center and then headed north for a few blocks. Before long, they arrived in front of a narrow two-story brick house. It had white shutters and a huge American flag waving from the second story.

"I'm so excited!" Emilia said. "We're studying the Revolutionary War in history class at the moment. Being in Philadelphia right now is perfect!"

"I bet this is even better than reading about it in a book," Dad said.

"I've heard of Betsy Ross," Zia said to Emilia. "But I don't know much about her."

"She was a seamstress and upholstery maker here in Philadelphia in the late seventeen and early eighteen hundreds," Emilia explained. "Her family claims that she was the first person to sew the American flag and present it to George Washington, but now there's a lot of debate about whether or not that's true. There just isn't much information to back it up."

"But this house is historic either way," Alfie added, studying the old exterior. "It says here that the front part of the house was built around 1740 with the back section added ten to twenty years later."

"Yes, I'd say that makes it historic, all right," Dad agreed.

Mom gave Alfie and Emilia money to buy tickets.

Emma led the way to purchase them.

"Good morning, Emma," the woman at the ticket counter said. "How are things at the Liberty Hotel?"

"Hi, Mrs. Wells," Emma responded. "They're ... fine. How are you?"

"Busy! But good," Mrs. Wells replied. "Let me just add the discount to your ticket price, and you'll be all set."

"Thank you," Alfie said, handing her the money.

"Everybody knows your hotel!" Emilia remarked.

Emma smiled. "We send guests to all the historic spots, so they give us a discount."

The family made their way through the museum, looking at all the cool artifacts—maps, textiles, and furniture—and reading the important information about the house, Betsy Ross, and her family. Alfie couldn't believe how many children Betsy Ross had in her lifetime. Sometimes having one sibling was enough of a challenge!

When they were done, they waited outside for Emilia,

who was still taking in every detail of the house.

"The house was restored in the 1930s," Emilia told them when she finally emerged. "And they've done lots of additions and improvements since then, thanks to the special groups in Philly."

"It's so important to preserve the past," Zia agreed.

"Well, what should we do next?" Dad asked.

"I thought we might go to the Italian Market on Ninth Street," Emma said.

"That sounds right up our alley," Mom said.

"I loved the Italian Market when I visited," Zia added. "How fun to go back!"

"It's in South Philly, where my grandma lives," said Emma. "That's traditionally the Italian section of the city, but now it's full of people and food from all over the world."

"Cool," Alfie said.

Dad hailed a minivan cab that could fit all of them, and they climbed inside. After a short ride, the cab pulled up to the curb in front of what Alfie assumed was the Italian Market. It was a collection of outdoor food and market stalls lining the busy street. They hopped out of the cab and walked along the sidewalk, taking it all in.

There were fruit and vegetable stands, cheese and meat stalls, spices, fresh Italian pasta, seafood vendors, ice-cream stalls, and bakeries—so many delicious-looking, and-smelling, foods. Each storefront was plastered in menus and posters, and local vendors passed out free samples to the crowd. Alfie tried a sample of fresh ricotta ravioli, a taste of strawberry buttermilk ice cream, and a square of extra-dark chocolate with cherries in it. Everything was delicious!

When they passed the meat market, Emma stopped to talk to the butcher. "Hi, Sam," she said. "I have a list from my mom to drop off. She said she'd pick it up tomorrow if that's okay with you."

"No problem, Emma," Sam replied. "Anything for my friends at the Liberty Hotel."

As they passed the cheese stall, the worker there
called Emma over. "We just got in that new goat's milk
cheese I was telling your mom about last week," the
woman said, handing a package to Emma. "Take this
home and tell me what you think!"

"Thanks, Alice. I will!" Emma smiled.

"You know everybody in town!" Emilia remarked.

"We shop at all the local markets in Philly and try to support as many other small family businesses as we can," Emma said.

"That's wonderful," Zia said. "And the food is so much fresher and more authentic!"

"For sure!" Emma agreed. But soon, a frown took over her face. "I just hope we can keep the hotel and restaurant up and running and stay in business!"

"You will," Emilia said gently.

"Well, all this talk of food is making me hungry!" Alfie said, trying to lighten the mood. He realized it had been a while since he'd eaten breakfast. He looked around at all the restaurants nearby. There was Mexican food, Vietnamese food, Korean barbecue, and Middle Eastern food all right near the market.

A smile spread across Emma's face. "How about a cheesesteak?"

"Finally!" Alfie responded, proudly showing off his

T-shirt. "I'm not totally sure what that is, but I like cheese and I like steak, so it has to be good!"

"Here's my chance to try an authentic Philly cheesesteak!" Dad chimed in.

"Great!" Emma said. "It's just a short walk away."

Emma led them south on Ninth Street. After a few blocks, they walked by a park and sports field. Nearby there were crowds of people gathered in front of two restaurants that sat across the street from each other.

"It's a huge debate in Philly as to which place is better. I've never been able to decide for myself," Emma explained.

"Why don't Mauricio, Arianna, and I get sandwiches from this one, and you kids can try the other one?" Zia suggested.

"Sounds good!" Emilia said.

Dad gave them some money, and they went to wait in line.

Alfie studied the menu. "So, what should I get?"

"A traditional cheesesteak is just thinly sliced steak on a long roll with cheese. You can  also get sautéed onions and peppers if you want," Emma replied. "Usually the choice is between provolone cheese and Cheez Whiz. I always get mine with Whiz."

"That's like the cheese sauce I had with my pretzel yesterday, right?" Alfie asked.

"Yep!"

"I'm definitely getting that," Alfie said.

"I'll have mine with provolone cheese and peppers," Emilia said.

Emma ordered for them, and before long, they were each presented with a huge sandwich packed with steak and cheese. They sat down at an outdoor table to eat their food.

Alfie took a giant bite, and Cheez Whiz dripped from his chin. The bread was soft and chewy, and the steak with the rich cheese sauce was a delicious mix. "Yum!" he said between bites.

Emilia put a little ketchup on her sandwich and then took a bite. She nodded vigorously. "So good!" she said. "Want to try mine, Alfie?"

"Sure!" Alfie said, taking a big bite of Emilia's sandwich. "Mmmmm. That's good, too! The peppers are so sweet. I like them."

"Me too!" Emilia added, taking back her sandwich.

"So, what's your favorite thing about living in a hotel?" Alfie asked Emma.

Emma put down her cheesesteak. "Definitely all the interesting people I meet!" she said.

"You've probably met people from all over the world!" Emilia said. "I would love that."

"I have." Emma grinned.

"What's your least favorite thing?" Alfie asked.

Emma sighed. "Probably all the problems we've been having, and that developer who keeps coming around. It seems like as soon as he showed up, that's when all our problems started. I know my parents are really stressed about all the repair costs. And I just can't bear to think of losing the hotel like that."

After a minute, Emilia spoke up—a smile growing on her face. "Well, I might have an idea."

A thought had just been running through Alfie's mind at the same time. "I've got one, too," he chimed in, excited to share it.

Chapter 10

Back at the hotel, everybody gathered in the restaurant dining room, eager to hear the ideas that Alfie and Emilia had.

"We visited the Betsy Ross House today," Emilia explained to Emma's parents. "And it got me thinking about historic buildings. No one would ever dream of tearing down that house, because it's a historic landmark."

"Of course not," Ann said.

"So why can't the Liberty Hotel be a landmark, too?" Emilia asked. "It's an old building with tons of interesting history, and it's right in the middle of the most historic part of Philadelphia!"

"That's true . . . ," John said, processing what Emilia was saying.

"So you should apply to become a landmarked building! That way no developer can come and tear it down. And maybe more people will want to stay here once they know how special it is," Emilia said all in one breath. Alfie could see how excited she was. It really was a great idea!

"Maybe that could work!" Emma said, getting excited, too.

"Absolutely," Ann agreed, looking at John. "I looked into it years ago, but I just didn't pursue it."

John nodded vigorously. "There's no reason not to try again!"

Emilia's face glowed.

"And what about you, Alfie?" Mom asked. "What was your idea?"

"At the Italian Market, I saw a poster for a fund-raising event, and I was thinking of the fund-raiser our band group had so that we could travel to special events around town. So, I wondered if maybe Emma and her family could have a fund-raiser to help them raise money for the renovations they need to do on the hotel."

"I'm not sure . . ." John hesitated. "I don't know if I'm very comfortable asking people for money."

"But if it's tied to getting historic status for your building, I think people will want to help," Mom argued.

"Plus," Alfie jumped in, "everyone we've met in the past couple of days loves this hotel *and* your family. If they knew what was going on, I bet they'd want to do something about it."

"We do know quite a few people in the community . . . ," John said.

"There has to be a historic society in Philadelphia," Zia added. "Maybe they would want to get involved!"

"Donatella's right," Ann said. "There's a huge chapter of the historical society here in Pennsylvania. They are always helping buildings that are in danger of being torn down."

"I'll call them!" Emilia jumped in. "I would *love* to talk to someone from the historical society!"

John shook his head and laughed. Then he looked at

Mom and Dad. "You've got two smart kids on your hands."

Dad put his arms around Alfie and Emilia's shoulders. "Yes, we do!" he said.

"I'm going to go get some paper so we can start planning," Emma said, dashing toward the lobby.

"And I'll throw together a few snacks in the kitchen and bring them out," Ann said.

Everybody else got to work setting the table at one of the bigger dining-room tables.

Soon Emma returned with a giant pad of paper, and Ann came out of the kitchen balancing a tray of snacks and drinks.

"I was just thinking," Ann said, "that it might be nice to host a big dinner or cocktail party here at the hotel for our fund-raiser."

"Yes!" Emma cheered. "We could sell tickets and plan a menu around a theme—something fun and festive with lots of food!"

"That sounds great," John replied, and everyone agreed.

"I would love to help make food for the party," Zia said.

"Oh, I would, too!" Mom chimed in. "What fun!"

"Fantastic!" Ann exclaimed.

Dad turned to John. "Are there any repairs or small fixes we can make before the fund-raiser? I'd be happy to help."

"That's so generous," John said. "It's really just the last couple of months that things have started to slip, and I can't understand it. I've had repairmen in here several times, and they either claim that nothing is wrong or that they've fixed the problem, but haven't."

"Well, we could go through the hotel floor by floor and make a list of things," Dad suggested.

"That's a great idea," John replied.

Alfie forgot about how tired he'd felt when they walked into the hotel. Now all he could think about was helping Emma and her parents put together the best possible plan to save their hotel. It just had to work!

Chapter 11

Along with Emma's family, the Bertolizzis worked for the rest of the afternoon to get the hotel and fund-raiser plans together. They decided to hold the fund-raiser in two days. Ann spoke to Mrs. Wells at the Betsy Ross House and learned that there was a meeting of the historical society in town, so they wanted to put together the fund-raiser as soon as possible so that some of the society members could attend.

Alfie followed his dad and John around the building, making a list of things that they'd need to tackle during the renovation. He liked seeing Emma's dad smile and get excited about the hotel again. The best of the day was seeing his dad, though. He had been so busy with work for such a long time that Alfie had forgotten how funny he was and how great he was at fixing things. He hummed while he worked and made Alfie and John laugh with silly jokes.

"Watch this, Alfie," Dad said, balancing a screwdriver on his nose. "I bet you didn't know your old man was so talented, did you?"

Alfie laughed. "I sure didn't!"

"Maybe we should have a talent show for a fund-raiser instead," Dad suggested.

"I think we should stick with a party," Alfie responded.

"All right. We'll do talents next time," Dad said with a wink.

Once they had gone floor to floor making a list of renovations, they met with the plumber and the electrician. Alfie thought both of them acted kind of strange. The electrician even got called away before they made it to the mechanical room to check on the wiring. He said there was an emergency and he'd have to come back later.

"Here's the pipe, right here," John told the plumber, pointing to the leak that had caused some of their guests to check out. "You said last week you replaced this piece!"

The plumber shifted from side to side and rubbed the back of his neck. "Uh, yeah . . . that's really weird. Let me go check something in my truck. I'll be right back."

The plumber practically bolted from the room. As the man tried to stuff a pen and notepad into his pocket, Alfie saw something fall to the floor. He walked over and picked it up. It was a business card. He figured he'd give it back to the plumber when he returned, but when John went out to check on him, his truck was gone.

After their odd encounters with the repairmen, Alfie, Dad, and John headed back to the restaurant dining room where everyone else was hard at work. Emilia and Ann focused on the historic landmark information while Emma, Mom, and Zia planned the fund-raiser menu.

Ann hung up the phone just as they entered the dining room. She and Emilia both had big grins on their faces. "They're going to send over a representative tomorrow morning before the big historical society meeting," Ann said. "They'll show us exactly what we need to do."

Emma's eyes grew wide. "That's fantastic!"

Emilia nodded excitedly. "And we both told her all about the fund-raiser. She said she'd be happy to spread the word at the meeting."

"Did you tell her that the party is in two days?" John asked, looking worried.

"Yep! And she didn't think that would be a problem. She said people would be happy gathering at short notice for a great cause."

Mom squeezed Emilia into a hug. "Well done, you two!" she said. Ann beamed at them both.

"It's all coming together!" Emma clapped excitedly. "We're not going to have to worry about that developer for much longer!"

Ann stood up. "Well, I don't know about the rest of you, but I could use a dinner break! Let me see what I can find in the kitchen."

"I'll help!" Zia said, following Ann.

While they waited for dinner to be served, Alfie, Emma, and Emilia worked on making posters they could hang around the neighborhood to advertise the fundraiser.

"What's going to be on the menu?" Alfie asked.

"We decided to make it a more fun and casual cocktail party—lots of finger foods and appetizers that really represent Philly," Emma told him.

"Like cheesesteaks and pretzels?" Emilia asked.

"Exactly! But we'll do cheesesteak sliders and pretzel

bites with different dipping sauces."

"Yum!" Alfie said. He wanted more of everything they'd tried so far in Philadelphia. "What else?"

"We're going to do some fresh vegetable and fruit trays with what's in season at the farmers' markets. Then we're going to make some classic Philadelphia Italian dishes, like Stromboli and tomato pie," Emma continued.

"Is tomato pie like pizza?" Alfie asked.

"It is," answered Emma. "It's a Sicilian-style pizza that doesn't have any cheese."

Alfie frowned. "That doesn't sound very exciting."

Emma laughed. "It's actually really good. The crust is kind of like focaccia bread, and it has a yummy, thick tomato-sauce base."

"It sounds good to me!" Emilia said.

A bit later, Zia and Ann returned from the kitchen with serving trays of grilled chicken breast, sautéed vegetables, and roasted potatoes. It smelled delicious. Everyone dug in, talking excitedly about the plans.

Mom joined in talking about the menu for the fundraiser. "Emma also had the great idea to include an appetizer that's made with Philadelphia cream cheese."

Emma smiled. "Well, Zia helped me come up with the actual recipe. We're going to make mini smoked salmon finger sandwiches with herbed cream cheese."

"Wow!" Dad chimed in. "I hope we're invited!"

"Of course you are!" Emma laughed.

"It's going to be such fun!" Mom said.

Alfie and Emilia exchanged a glance and smiled at each other. Mom was excited, too. They hadn't seen their parents this relaxed in a long time. And neither of them had brought up work at all. Alfie secretly wished they could stay in Philadelphia—especially if it meant his parents would stay this way.

Chapter 12

The next morning, everyone was up bright and early to continue preparations for the fund-raiser. They ate a quick breakfast, and then Alfie and Emma set out to hang their posters around the neighborhood. Emilia stayed behind, eager to meet the woman from the historical society and hear all about the process for making the Liberty Hotel a landmark.

It was another beautiful late spring day, and the morning sun was bright and warm. Alfie and Emma covered the neighborhood hanging posters. Then they took a smaller version of their best poster to a print shop to make flyers and postcards. After that, they went around to local businesses, asking them to post the flyers or leave a stack of postcards someplace where people could grab one.

"Of course!" the owner of the local dry cleaner told them. "Anything for the Liberty Hotel."

"I've always loved that beautiful old hotel," said the woman at the coffee shop across the street, gazing out the window at the building. "And the fund-raiser sounds like fun. Tell your parents my husband and I will definitely be there!"

Each business they stopped in was more excited than the last. Everybody loved Emma and her family, and cared about what happened to the hotel. No one wanted to see it go.

Alfie and Emma were excited and feeling positive when they headed back to the hotel empty-handed. They found Ann and Mom together at the reception desk. Ann was on the phone, and Mom was on a laptop. They both looked very focused.

"What's going on?" Alfie asked.

"Ticket sales for the fund-raiser are already starting to come in!" Mom said with a big grin on her face. "Wherever you've put the posters and flyers, it's definitely working!"

Emma bounced on her toes. "I can't wait!"

They found Emilia, Dad, and John in the dining room with the woman from the historical society. Emilia looked just as pleased as they were.

"Everything looks great," the woman told them as she stood up from her chair. "The Liberty Hotel seems to meet all the criteria we need. I'm going to get the paperwork submitted this afternoon, and we'll have a final answer to you shortly."

"Thank you so much," John said, shaking her hand vigorously.

"And I'll tell all our members about the fund-raiser," the woman turned to say as she walked out of the dining room. "I know everyone will want to come out and support the cause."

"It's really happening," Emma said, a little breathless.

"We're not out of the woods yet," John replied, crossing his fingers. "We need to wait to hear back. Hopefully they'll approve our paperwork."

"Of course they will. I can tell!" Emma said, putting her arm around her dad's waist.

Just then, Zia rushed out of the kitchen with a piece of paper in her hand. "I'm so glad you're back. Can the three of you go to the Italian Market with this list? These are most of the ingredients we need to make food for the party."

"Definitely!" Alfie said. He was happy to have a reason to go back there and explore more.

"Great!" Zia smiled. "Just call us if you have any questions. And here's some money for food and cab fare. Ann said you can arrange to have all the food delivered tomorrow morning."

"Yes," Emma said, "we do that all the time for the restaurant."

Alfie, Emilia, and Emma hurried out of the hotel and

in the direction of the Italian Market. "We should make a quick stop on the way," Emma said. "You'll want to see this."

They walked along South Street, and soon they came across a gap between two buildings. The side of one of the buildings and the whole front of the other was covered in mosaics. There was a gate and a shorter wall in between that was also covered in bits of broken tile and brightly colored glass—all in interesting and artistic patterns.

"This is Philadelphia's Magic Gardens," Emma told them.

"Wow!" Alfie said, taking it all in. "Someone made all this?"

"Yep," Emma responded. "An artist did. It took him over fourteen years." Emma pushed open the gate, and they walked inside.

Glass pieces glinted in the sun like silver, while the rainbow of other colors—bold blues, greens, yellows, oranges, and reds—seemed to dance all around them.

"There are so many different materials," Emilia said, running her hand along the wall. "Bike wheels, glass jars, china plates—all kinds of things!"

"And even the floor is all mosaics," Alfie remarked as they climbed a tiled stairway to another level. "It's so cool."

"I thought you would like it," Emma said.

Alfie, Emilia, and Emma finished their tour and popped back onto South Street to continue toward the Italian Market. When they got there, they looked at Zia's list and bought fresh ingredients from all kinds of vendors, some of whom they'd met with Emma already. They posted flyers and postcards advertising the fundraiser at each stall they visited. Everyone they talked to was really supportive and happy to spread the word.

Once they'd finished, Emma led the way to a local farmers' market. They handed out the rest of their flyers and then ordered all the fresh fruits and vegetables they needed. Alfie couldn't believe the number of people Emma knew at that market, too! *Philadelphia really is the City of Brotherly Love*, he decided.

After the groceries were purchased, Emma hailed a

cab, and they buzzed along the city streets back toward the Liberty Hotel.

"Thanks for showing us the Magic Gardens," Emilia said. "You've been such an amazing host. We've seen so many cool things."

"Thank *you* for all your help!" Emma said.

"I'm so excited about it all!" Emilia continued. "Working with the woman from the historical society was amazing. I think I might want to do that some day."

Emma nodded, but her smile faded a little bit. "I love our plan, and people seem to be responding to it. I just hope it's enough. The thought of selling to that condo developer . . ." Emma shuddered. "There is just something about that guy . . ."

Alfie got a weird feeling in his stomach. "What did you say the developer's name was?"

"I'll have to ask my dad to be sure, but I think it was Ray something . . ."

"Ray Stevens?" Alfie asked.

"That's it. How did you know?"

Alfie pulled the business card from his pocket. "The plumber dropped this when he ran out of the hotel yesterday. Maybe he's working with the developer, and that's why none of the repairs were done right!"

Emma studied the card with wide eyes. "We have to tell my dad!"

When they reached the hotel, they hurried inside. Emma passed the business card to her dad and told him what Alfie had discovered.

"Well, that explains quite a bit!" John said, studying the card. "I knew those repairs hadn't been done correctly."

"And those repairmen were acting so strange yesterday," Alfie added. "Like they couldn't wait to get out of here!"

"That's right," John agreed. "I had a feeling something was off at the time, but I didn't know what it was."

"Good detective work, Alfie," Dad said, ruffling his

hair. "This is a really, really big deal."

Alfie smiled.

"I'm going to make a few phone calls," John said, hurrying into his office.

"Where are Mom and Zia?" Emilia asked. "We have to tell them, too!"

"They're in the kitchen," Dad answered.

Everybody went into the kitchen to fill in Ann, Mom, and Zia on the big discovery. Ann and Zia made sandwiches while they talked. They were just sitting down to eat when John rushed into the room. "I called the plumber, and he confessed to working with Ray Stevens."

"I knew it!" Alfie cried.

"He said Mr. Stevens paid him double to do shoddy work, but he's been feeling bad about it and doesn't want to be involved anymore."

"Well, I should hope not!" Ann said.

"So then I called my old college buddy at the

Philadelphia Daily News," John continued, "and he's going to run a story about the developer. He's already been writing for months about all the buildings that have been torn down around the city. He said almost all of them have been thanks to Ray Stevens. And every time he tries to talk to Mr. Stevens, he avoids my friend and won't return his calls. He wants to talk to you for the story, Alfie, since you're the one who put the pieces together with the repairmen."

"Okay," Alfie said. His heart beat in his throat. He had never talked to a reporter before. He was nervous and excited all at the same time. Dad squeezed his shoulder.

"And the plumber has already agreed to speak with my friend, too," John added.

"That's great!" Dad said.

"So grab your sandwich and come with me," John told Alfie with a smile. "You've got an interview to do!"

"Right now?" Alfie asked. Suddenly he didn't feel very hungry.

"Yep!" John said. "My friend wants to get started on the story as soon as possible. We can call him from my office."

Alfie looked at his dad. Dad smiled and stood up, ready to follow Alfie and John out of the room.

"You'll do great, *ragazzo!*" Zia encouraged.

"Way to go, Alfie!" Emilia called out.

Alfie felt his stomach drop as he walked out of the dining room.

✳   ✳   ✳

In the hotel office, John called his friend at the newspaper, Conrad, and put the phone on speaker.

"It's nice to meet you, Alfie," Conrad said. "Can you all hear me okay?"

"Loud and clear," John answered, flashing Alfie a thumbs-up.

Dad put his arm around his son.

"Great!" Conrad continued. "So, Alfie. Let's jump right in. Can you tell me about what happened with the plumber?"

"Well," Alfie started, nervously, "I thought he was acting strange when he came to look at the pipes. He seemed nervous and uncomfortable—kind of like how I get before a math test."

Everybody laughed. Alfie began to relax.

"Then he made an excuse about needing to go to his truck and rushed out of the room. As he was leaving, something fell out of his pocket. I picked it up thinking I'd give it to him when he came back, but he never did. The thing I picked up was a business card for Ray Stevens."

"But you didn't tell John or your dad about it?"

"No, I didn't think it was a big deal. I put it in my pocket and forgot about it until today, when Emma was talking about the developer. Suddenly, it all made sense."

"I bet it did," Conrad replied, chuckling. "Now, what happened next?"

"Emma brought the business card to her dad, and we told him the story. Then he called you."

"That's fantastic," Conrad said. "What a huge discovery you made!"

Alfie beamed.

"I'm going to get started on the rest of my research, but I'll let you know if I have any other questions for you," Conrad said.

"Okay!"

"Thanks for talking to me, Alfie. I wouldn't have much of a story without you."

"You're welcome," Alfie said. His nervousness about the interview had melted away. Now he just felt excited!

Chapter 13

Alfie and Emilia woke up the next morning feeling a little more rested. Alfie thought he'd be wide awake after the thrill of being interviewed for a newspaper article, but he was so tired from the busy day that he'd crashed right away. He could still hear creaks and noises throughout the night, but now he was more used to the sounds of the old building.

When Mom, Dad, and Zia were ready, they all headed down to the lobby and found Emma at the reception desk, helping her dad sort through a stack of paperwork.

"Good morning!" Emma and her dad said.

"Morning!" the Bertolizzis replied.

"Great job answering those questions yesterday," John said to Alfie. "My friend called this morning. He worked on the article all night long. It's going to be posted online tonight and run as a feature in the morning edition tomorrow!"

"Wow!" Alfie said. "I didn't think it would be done that quick!"

"When there's breaking news, you have to act fast," Mom said.

"That's right!" John nodded. "I'll let you know as soon as the story is out."

"Okay, thanks," Alfie said.

"We got another stack of flyers and postcards from the printer," Emma told them. "I thought we could go hang them around the Philadelphia Museum of Art and then stop in for a quick visit."

"That's a fabulous idea!" Zia said.

"Yeah, cool!" Emilia added.

After a light breakfast in the restaurant, they found

another minivan cab and hopped in. The museum was in the opposite direction of the other sites they'd visited so far—on the edge of the Schuylkill River. Alfie was excited. They hadn't visited a museum on any of their other Zia adventures.

They arrived in front of a tan brick building with tall Greek columns and wide steps leading up to it.

"I recognize these steps!" Dad said.

"You do?" Alfie asked. "I thought you'd never been to Philly before?"

"I haven't, but I've seen them in *Rocky*," Dad explained.

"They're very famous because of that," Emma said as they climbed out of the taxi. "There's a statue of Rocky right over here. I'll show you!"

"Who's Rocky?" Alfie asked, still confused.

Dad put his arm around Alfie's shoulder. "He's a boxer played by the actor Sylvester Stallone in a series of movies. The original movie was way before your time, but it's a classic."

The family stood in front of the bronze statue of a man in boxing shorts and gloves holding his arms in the air in victory. Dad mimicked the pose, and everybody laughed. Zia snapped a picture with her phone.

"Come on," Dad said to Alfie. "Let's race to the top of the steps!"

Alfie laughed again, thinking Dad was joking, but then he took off at a run. Alfie exchanged a surprised look with Emilia and then hurried to catch up, a big grin on his face. He hadn't seen Dad act this silly in a long time!

Dad beat Alfie to the top, but Alfie was right behind him. Alfie doubled over, trying to catch his breath as Mom, Zia, Emilia, and Emma walked up behind them, still laughing.

"There are seventy-two steps," Emma said.

"That's . . . a lot," Dad wheezed.

Once Alfie and Dad were able to breathe again, they all walked past the fountain in the center of the courtyard and into the museum. Mom went to pay for their tickets.

"I'll go with you," Emma told her. "We get a discount here, too."

Mom and Emma went to the ticket counter while the rest of the family grabbed museum guides. When they came back, Emma was beaming.

"They agreed to hang up our flyers," Emma said. "Now everyone who visits the museum will know about our fund-raiser!"

"And we got discounts," Mom said, smiling. She passed out the tickets, and they all stopped to look at the map. Everybody wanted to see something different. Alfie wanted to go to the modern art rooms and galleries. Emilia decided to see the Impressionists collection. Emma and Zia headed off to a special pottery exhibit, and Mom and Dad wanted to check out the photography collection. They all agreed to meet back in the lobby an hour and a half later.

Alfie wandered through the wide-open gallery rooms, looking at the modern art paintings and sculptures. He liked the splatter-and-drip paintings of Jackson Pollock. They reminded him of some of his art projects from second grade! When the time was up, everybody gathered again and talked about what they'd seen.

"The Claude Monet paintings were my favorite,"

Emilia said. "I wish we had visited his gardens in France. His water lilies are so beautiful."

"Maybe one day, *bambina*," Mom said, winking at Dad.

"I liked the pieces that looked like comics," Alfie said. "Those were cool!"

"I thought the Wedgwood collection from England was really impressive," Zia said. "All those old plates and dishes are beautiful."

They walked outside and took in the view of the city from the top of the steps. The river looked beautiful from so high up. Then they wandered around the grounds a bit, looking at various statues. "I love it here!" Emilia gushed. "I would come here every day if we lived in Philadelphia."

"It's one of my favorite places," Emma agreed.

"But what should we do with the rest of our flyers?" Alfie asked.

"We can head down to Fairmount Avenue," Emma said. "There are lots of restaurants and shops that will probably let us hang flyers and leave postcards."

"And maybe eat lunch," Alfie added, making everyone laugh as usual.

Once they'd finished advertising the fund-raiser, Emma took them to a sandwich shop that served traditional Italian hoagies. Alfie got one with ham, salami, and provolone. It was drizzled with an Italian dressing and had shredded lettuce and tomato on it. The roll was similar to the bread from yesterday's cheesesteak: slightly chewy and very delicious. They also each picked out a bottle of old-fashioned soda. Alfie chose root beer, while Emilia chose black cherry, and Emma picked ginger ale. Mom and Dad both had vanilla cream, and Zia had orange cream.

"Philadelphia is the birthplace of soda, too," Zia said. "I learned that from my friends last time I visited."

"So many good things originated here!" Alfie said.

"Pretzels and soda. This is my kind of city!"

"Don't forget marshmallow Peeps and Peanut Chews. Those are made here in Pennsylvania, too," Mom said.

"I love Peeps!" Alfie said.

"Gross," Emilia responded, making a face.

"There's also a brand of snack cakes and doughnuts called Tastykakes," Emma added. "They're so good."

"That does sound tasty!" Alfie said.

"And my favorite: Hershey's chocolate," Mom chimed in. "That's made in Pennsylvania as well."

"That's another place I wouldn't mind touring," Emilia said. "A chocolate factory!"

"We'll have to do that next time," Mom said. "For now, I think we should head back to the hotel and help Ann and John with party plans!"

"Good idea," Zia said. "There's still so much to do."

"I hope we can sell enough tickets," Emma said as they looked for a cab. "We've already bought all the food and everything."

"Everyone we've talked to has been really excited about it," Alfie said. "I think we'll sell plenty of tickets."

"I hope you're right," Emma responded.

As soon as Emma and the Bertolizzis stepped into the hotel, Ann and John rushed to them.

"You're not going to believe it!" Ann said, smiling. "Tickets for the fund-raiser are completely sold out!"

Chapter 14

"How do I look?" Dad asked Mom.

Mom hurried over and straightened his tie. "Very sharp," she said.

"Everyone looks so nice," Zia added.

They were all gathered in Mom and Dad's room, getting ready for the fund-raiser party. Mom and Zia had taken Alfie and Emilia shopping earlier that day to get new clothes for the big night. Emilia turned in a circle, admiring her new red dress.

"We should get downstairs," Zia said. "I want to make sure Ann doesn't feel too overwhelmed in the kitchen."

"Yes, let's," Mom agreed, heading for the door.

"We're helping Emma check names off the list and do the coat check," Alfie said. "But after that, we'll come help in the kitchen."

"Great!" Zia said.

As soon as they made it downstairs, a few early guests arrived. Emilia and Emma checked the guests in while Alfie hung coats behind the

reception desk. Everyone was dressed in fancy cocktail attire, and some of them looked very important.

When the arrivals slowed down, Alfie peeked around the hotel. Ann, Mom, and Zia had done a fantastic job decorating the space. Small twinkle lights hung around the dining room with candles flickering on all the tables. The vases from the seller at the Italian Market had arrived, and fresh flowers were sprinkled around the room. Some of the bigger dining tables had been replaced with high standing tables where guests gathered with their drinks and appetizers. Waiters and waitresses in matching shirts who were hired for the event circulated through the space, passing out the delicious-looking bites. Alfie couldn't wait to try everything they'd made!

Once most of the guests had arrived, Emma's dad took over the ticket table so that Emma, Emilia, and Alfie could go help in the kitchen. They darted through the crowd and opened the kitchen door, eager to see how things were going.

Zia, Mom, and Ann rushed around. There were several other people from the waitstaff company helping fill trays and serving platters.

"What can we do to help?" Emma asked, slipping an apron over her head. Alfie and Emilia washed their hands at the sink.

Zia pointed to an empty tray. "We need another vegetable tray. Alfie and Emilia, can you fill the tray with veggies while Emma dishes up more spinach dip?"

"Sure!" Alfie and Emilia said together. They also put on aprons to keep their clothes clean, and then got to work on the tray.

Mom wiped her hands on a towel and came over to see how things were going. "You two look like complete pros in the kitchen!"

"We've had lots of practice," Emilia said.

"Yep," Alfie agreed. "We helped throw a party in New Orleans and another one in Maui. And we passed out samples at a food festival in Miami. It's so much fun!"

"I'm so impressed," Mom said.

With all of them working in the kitchen, it didn't take long to get ahead on preparations. Soon there was enough food ready for the servers to bring out so they could take a break and join the party.

Alfie, Emilia, and Emma took off their aprons and headed eagerly into the dining room. Alfie's breath caught in his throat when he opened the door. The hotel dining room was full of people! He knew they'd sold all the tickets, but he'd had a hard time imagining that the space would be totally full. Everybody looked like they were having a great time. Music played over the sound system, and people mingled and laughed and, most important, ate lots of food!

"I'm going to find the woman from the historical

society," Emilia said, disappearing into the crowd. "I want to see if the society has made a final decision."

"And I see a couple of friends," Emma said. "I'll be back."

Alfie moved through the crowd, accepting appetizers from every tray that passed. Before long, he had a cocktail napkin piled with goodies. Dad emerged holding a similarly loaded napkin. He and Alfie laughed when they saw each other.

"I think things are going well," Dad said, popping a pretzel bite into his mouth.

Alfie nodded, his mouth too full of spinach dip to respond.

John made his way through the guests and over to Alfie and Dad. "Mauricio, I wanted to introduce you to Tom Larsen. He's a contractor, and he's offered to take a look at the building free of charge and then give an estimate on the work that needs to be done."

"Nice to meet you, Tom," Dad said, shaking his hand.

Tom nodded. "My wife is on the board for the historical society. After she told me the story about John's building and I read the newspaper article, I knew I wanted to get involved. I specialize in old buildings like this one, so I know I'm up for the challenge."

"That's fantastic," Dad said. "John and his family care so much about the Liberty Hotel. It's a beautiful building."

"My wife and I have always admired the Liberty from afar. We'll do everything we can!" Tom said.

"The newspaper article is the talk of the party!" John told Alfie and Dad. "No one can believe Ray Stevens got away with what he did for so long."

"Well, not anymore," Dad said. "Alfie made sure of that!"

Alfie beamed.

"That reminds me," John said. "I think it's time for me to make a toast!"

John made his way to the front of the restaurant and

switched on a microphone. The room fell silent. "Excuse me, everyone," he said. "I just wanted to thank you all for gathering to celebrate our historic hotel. Your support means the world to me and my family. And I want to give special thanks to our new friends, the Bertolizzis. None of this would have been possible without them." John raised his glass in the air. "Cheers to friends, old and new, and to our wonderful historical community!"

"Cheers!" the party replied.

Emilia cut through the crowd and stood next to Alfie. "Pretty fun party, huh?"

"Yeah!"

"Have you tried the mini cheesecakes Emma made?" Emilia asked.

"There's mini cheesecake?" Alfie asked, looking around.

Emilia laughed and extended her napkin. "Don't worry. I got an extra one. It's *so* good!"

Alfie took a bite of the rich dessert with a glazed

strawberry on top. It was the perfect mix of sweet and creamy. "I'm going to need another one of those!"

Emilia giggled again. "Follow me."

Once Alfie had his fill of cheesecake, he and Emilia found Zia talking to an older couple. "These are my Italian friends who live here!" Zia said, introducing them.

"It's so nice to meet Donatella's family," they said. "We're glad you're enjoying our adopted city."

"We love it here!" Alfie replied. "It's been a really fun trip."

When the party started to wind down, Alfie and Emilia went back to the lobby to help with the coat check. Alfie was surprised by how many people gave them tips. He wasn't expecting that. Sometimes people handed them a five- or ten-dollar bill! Emma found a big glass jar to put all the money in.

"We're raising even more money for the hotel!" Alfie said.

When the last coat was taken from the rack, Alfie,

Emma, and Emilia went back into the dining room. Alfie expected to see plates and cups and leftover food everywhere, but the waitstaff was moving quickly through the space, clearing and cleaning as they went. Back in the kitchen, it didn't look too bad, either.

"We planned so well with the food that we really don't have that many leftovers," Ann said. "Thanks to Zia's expert party-planning skills."

Zia smiled. "I've had years of experience throwing parties. I'm so glad nothing was wasted."

Dad and John came into the kitchen. "Well, that's everybody!" John said. "I think I'd better go to bed before I decide to just sleep here on the kitchen floor."

Ann nodded. "I agree. Let's leave the rest of the cleanup for the morning."

Just then, Alfie realized how tired he was. He sleepily followed his family upstairs and collapsed onto his bed. He had just enough energy to take his shoes off before he fell fast asleep.

Chapter 15

The next morning, the two families gathered in the dining room for breakfast and to recap the evening.

"I still can't believe what an amazing turnout we had," Ann said. "I saw people I haven't seen in years!"

"It really was something," John agreed. "We had some friends and family come all the way from New York and Washington, DC, to support us. And on such short notice!"

"How wonderful!" said Zia. "I met so many interesting people."

"And it was nice to meet your Italian friends, too, Zia," Alfie said.

"Yes!" Mom jumped in. "I loved talking with them about Naples."

"I still wish the woman from the historical society had given us an answer," Emilia said.

"It's funny that you mention that," John said slyly, sipping his coffee. "She already called this morning and said she'd be sending over a draft of the paperwork. She told me that the overwhelming support from the community made it clear that we'll get our landmark status without any sort of problem."

Both families erupted in celebration.

"That's wonderful!" Zia exclaimed.

"Bravissimo!" Dad joined in.

Ann and Emma got up from their seats to hug John. He squeezed them tight. Everyone breathed a sigh of relief.

"But we couldn't have done it without your brilliant idea, Emilia," John added. "And your idea, Alfie."

Emilia and Alfie smiled, turning bright red.

"We had several extra donations from some pretty major families and businesses in our neighborhood," Ann added. "We far exceeded our fund-raising goal. And we've come up with a few more fund-raising ideas. They will be smaller events—nothing as involved as last night, but I think we can get the funds we need to make this hotel as great as it used to be!"

"I'm so excited!" Emma said. "I can't wait to see it once the renovations are done. And then we can work on making the restaurant menu even better, too. I already have tons of new ideas!"

"You're a very talented chef," Zia told Emma. "I have no doubt your new menu is going to be really exciting."

"Maybe we can send it to you for your tips and suggestions?" Emma asked.

Zia beamed. "I would love that!"

"And not only that, but the newspaper article about Ray Stevens has sparked a citywide investigation into his business dealings," John said. "Thanks to Alfie's quick thinking, a few other old buildings just might be saved, too!"

Mom squeezed Alfie into a hug. He grinned.

"We really couldn't have done any of this without you," Ann told the Bertolizzis. "Your support has been incredible. How can we ever repay you?"

"Well, I, for one, would love to come back after the renovations are complete, so how about saving us a couple of rooms?" Dad said.

"Absolutely!" John agreed. "You're welcome anytime. It'll be our treat. Perhaps we'll have another party once everything is complete."

"Oh, can we?" Emma asked.

"I think that's a great idea," Ann said.

Alfie sat back and took in the smiling faces of his family and their new friends. It felt great to help Emma and her parents with something so important. And who knows? Maybe he'd add *detective* to his list of possible careers!

Chapter 16

Later that day, Mom and Dad called Alfie and Emilia into their room.

"We thought we'd have a special birthday dinner for Alfie tonight," Mom said.

"Even though your birthday will still be a couple of days away when we get home, more than a few days have passed here, so we think a celebration is in order!" Dad added.

"Awesome!" Alfie said. He certainly wasn't going to argue with celebrating his birthday twice. And he remembered that they did the same for Emilia when they were in Rio. He was excited to have his turn.

"Where are we going?" Emilia asked.

"We're going to my friends' Italian restaurant in South Philly!" Zia said. "And we thought it would be fun if Emma and her parents joined us."

"Yes!" Alfie cheered. Even though they had traveled to so many places and experienced so many different foods, Italian food would always be his favorite. And he couldn't think of a better way to celebrate than with their new friends.

When they reached the restaurant, Zia's friends greeted them. A special large table had been set up in the back just for them. There was some confetti sprinkled on the table and a big balloon tied to the back of each chair. "Wow!" Alfie said, taking the seat at the head of the table.

"Happy birthday, Alfie," Emma said, placing a card and a wrapped gift on the table in front of him.

"Thanks, Emma," Alfie replied. "You didn't have to get me a gift!"

"It's just something small from a store in the

neighborhood," she said, her cheeks flushing pink.

Alfie read the card and unwrapped the present. It was a music book of songs that featured drum solos. "How cool!"

"They're all songs that are supposed to be good for drummers," Emma told him.

"That's awesome. Thanks, Emma!"

Before long, big plates of pasta, sautéed vegetables, and baskets of bread arrived at the table. Alfie dug in happily.

"Alfie, you still haven't told us what you want for your birthday," Mom said. "Your party is coming up fast when we get home!"

"We've been so busy and we're having so much fun here that I guess I really haven't thought about any other gifts," Alfie replied. "I just wish Zia didn't have to go."

Zia smiled and patted Alfie's hand.

"But I know you're ready for some new adventures of your own," Alfie said. "So it's okay."

"Thank you, *ragazzo*," Zia replied. "And I promise to visit again soon."

Dad pushed back from the table and patted his belly. "I'm going to need to work overtime at the gym after this vacation."

Everybody laughed.

"We have had so much good food while we've been here," Mom agreed, just as a tiramisu cake with lit candles arrived at the table.

The entire restaurant sang "Happy Birthday" to Alfie as he blew out his candles and made a wish.

"We should probably head back to the hotel," John said once everyone had finished their slices of tiramisu.

"Yes, we should," Ann added. "We've got a lot of work to do! I have a feeling we'll be taking new reservations in no time."

"I'm just so glad everything worked out!" Mom said. "Well, we won't keep you. Thanks again for joining us for dinner."

"Happy birthday!" Emma exclaimed.

"Thank you!" Alfie replied, brushing cocoa powder from his shirt.

"I could use a stroll around the neighborhood," Zia said. "I think I'm too full to go back to the hotel just yet."

"Yes! Let's walk around!" Emilia agreed.

The Bertolizzis thanked Zia's friends for the wonderful dinner and then wandered through the neighborhood, enjoying the light evening breeze. They walked down quiet side streets with small community gardens. People were walking their dogs and enjoying the night.

"Look, that bakery is still open," Dad said, pointing across the street. "Let's stop in."

"Mauricio." Mom gave him a stern look. "We've just eaten enough for a small army."

"There's always room for a little extra, right, kids?" Dad said with a wink.

"I couldn't agree more," Alfie said. "Besides, it's my pretend birthday!"

Zia and Mom laughed.

"It does look like a classic Italian bakery," Zia said.

"Oh, all right," Mom conceded.

They crossed the street and stepped into the small brightly lit bakery. Alfie took a deep breath, filling his nose with the smell of fresh sweet pastries. "What are you going to have?" he asked Emilia.

"There are so many choices!" she replied, scanning the case. "They even have *pizzelles*!"

"Those are beautiful," Mom said, leaning in close. "But look at the cannoli."

"That's what I want!" Alfie replied instantly, eyeing one with chocolate chips in the filling.

"Me too," Emilia said.

"That does look delicious . . . ," Zia agreed.

"Let's just share a couple," Mom suggested.

"Three cannoli with chocolate chips, please," Dad told the baker.

He put the cannoli in a pink box tied with white string and handed it across the counter with some napkins. The family went back outside to a table under the bakery sign to enjoy their Italian treat. Mom cut each one in half with a plastic knife.

Alfie took a bite of his half and let the thick cream settle on his tongue for a minute before crunching into one of the mini chocolate chips.

"I can't remember the last time I had one of these!" Mom said between bites.

"Maybe around Christmas last year?" Dad asked. "That night we had the neighbors over for dinner?"

"I think you're right!" Mom said.

"They brought those store-bought cannoli that were not very good, and we had to pretend to like them!" Alfie interjected.

Zia laughed.

Soon, Dad joined in. "They were pretty bad. Not like these!"

Just as Alfie took another bite of his dessert, he felt the air shift around him and his stomach whooshed forward. It was time to go home!

Chapter 17

It had been two days since the family returned from their Philadelphia adventure. Mom and Dad could not stop talking about all the fun they'd had. Neither could Alfie, Emilia, and Zia. It really had been an amazing trip.

Now Alfie stood at the picnic table in the backyard, surrounded by his friends from school and his soccer team. The table was piled high with gifts, food, and a big chocolate birthday cake.

He had one wrapped present left on the table. It was from Emilia and Zia. He tore open the paper and hefted out a huge, beautiful atlas. He loved it! He wanted to sit down and thumb through the thick pages right then and there, but he knew he'd better wait until later so his friends wouldn't get bored.

"Wow!" Alfie said. "Thanks so much! This is perfect."

"You're welcome," Emilia said, smiling.

"Use it wisely," Zia said with a wink.

"There's one more present," Mom announced. "But it's too big to move, so you'll have to find it in the garage."

Alfie grinned and ran inside the garage. His friends followed. There stood a brand-new drum kit with two new drumsticks wrapped in big red bows. "Cool!"

"That's awesome," Alfie's friend Daniel said.

"Yeah, that's a really good drum set," Charlie agreed, looking impressed.

"Thanks, Mom and Dad." Alfie smiled from ear to ear. "I love it!"

"Happy birthday, son," Dad said.

After they'd had their fill of birthday cake and snacks, Alfie and his friends played the new video game he'd gotten from Jackson. The afternoon flew by, and soon it was time for the parents to start arriving. Alfie stood by the front door and thanked all of his friends for coming. When the last friend had gone, he went into the kitchen to find Mom, Dad, and Zia cleaning up. Emilia was busy bringing in the rest of the gifts from the backyard.

"Thank you for everything," Alfie told them. "I had a great party!"

"I'm so glad," Mom said.

"I feel like our trip to Philadelphia was enough of a present, but then I got a party and all these great gifts, too!"

"Well, there's still one last thing," Dad said.

"What?" Alfie asked. He couldn't believe there was more.

Dad exchanged a look with Mom and Zia. "We've been

talking, and we've decided to start planning a big family vacation for later this summer."

"Really?" Emilia asked.

"Going to Philadelphia and spending time with you kids in a new city was really eye-opening for us," Mom said. "We loved having that time together to relax as a family. It was so great to see you and your sister in a new city. You're so independent!"

"It also made us realize what the three of you have been saying all along about us working too much," Dad added. "It's time to slow things down at the office."

"And start being more present at home," Mom continued. "We've already started brainstorming where we should go."

"Where have you been thinking?" Emilia asked excitedly.

"We're not quite sure yet," Dad said.

"But wherever it is, it's going to be somewhere that you can meet up with me out on my travels," Zia said.

"No way!" Alfie shouted. "That will be so much fun!"

"Will it be Naples?" Emilia asked. "We could see Enzo and Marco!"

"Yeah," Alfie said. "Or we could go back to the cooking school in Paris. I bet Monsieur DuBois would love to see us again!"

Emilia laughed.

"I think we should meet somewhere none of us have ever been," Zia said. "How's that for an adventure?"

Alfie looked at Mom and Dad, expecting them to seem unsure.

"I love that idea!" Mom said.

"I think we're up for the challenge," Dad agreed.

Alfie was surprised. Their trip to Philadelphia really had changed Mom and Dad. "This is the best birthday present I can think of!"

They all crowded together in a big group hug.

✳   ✳   ✳

The next morning, the family was up bright and early to

see Zia off on her travels. Dad hauled her two big suitcases out to the taxi.

"Are you sure you have everything?" Mom asked, her eyes misting over.

"Yes, Arianna. I'll be fine." Zia laughed. "I've done this hundreds of times, you know?"

"I know, I know," Mom said, giving Zia another hug.

"Your bags are in the car, Donatella," Dad said before squeezing Zia into a big hug himself.

Zia turned to Alfie and Emilia. Alfie felt a lump forming in his throat.

"I want you two to keep having adventures," Zia said. "Even if that means discovering new places right here in your hometown."

"Okay, Zia," Emilia said. "We will."

"And keep reading about and researching new places," Zia continued. "You never know where you might end up next!"

Alfie nodded. "At least we know we'll be seeing you in a couple of months."

"Yes, you will! I'll keep in close touch so we can decide soon where our meeting spot will be."

Zia smoothed down Emilia's hair. Emilia lunged forward and wrapped her in a tight squeeze. Then Zia kissed Alfie on the forehead before he did the same.

"See you soon, *mia famiglia*," Zia said, turning toward the door.

"Bye, Zia!" Emilia called.

"Arrivederci!" Alfie added.

They stood in the doorway and watched Zia get into

the cab. The cab backed out of the driveway, and Zia waved before disappearing down the street.

Alfie smiled. School would be ending soon, and before long, they'd be off on their family vacation. He couldn't wait to decide where they'd go. Alfie knew their next adventure might not be made from magic, but it would still be magical to them—all thanks to Zia.

A Note from Giada

After so many delicious adventures around the world—from Naples to New Orleans to Hong Kong—I knew that choosing the next great food destination for Recipe for Adventure would be tough. That's why I launched a nationwide contest with Penguin to give readers the chance to bring Alfie and Emilia to their favorite city! And after I pored over incredible submissions and sampled recipes from around the country, one fan and her hometown dish truly stood out. I was thrilled to send the Bertolizzis to the birthplace of America— Philadelphia!—to meet our winner, Emma, and sample her delicious Italian pizzelles! I hope you'll try her recipe for yourself and taste a bite of South Philly.

I recently visited Philly with Jade while I was on a book tour, and I was reminded of how much I love the city. From the abundance of history and iconic sights to the fantastic food around every corner, you can't go wrong with a visit. The city is a melting pot for some of the best cuisine . . . and that includes Italian! Thanks to awesome local farmers who create a fresh farm-to-table food scene, you can definitely get a taste of Italy in Philadelphia. And let's not forget to mention the Philly cheesesteaks! Besides the food, there was enough culture, theater, and museums in Philadelphia to keep me and Jade exploring for days. May the Liberty Bell keep ringing until we're back!